The Tindims
and the
TURTLE TANGLE

Mother-daughter duo,
Sally Gardner and Lydia Corry
are keen conservationists. Sally
is a Costa and Carnegie-winning
author and Lydia's *Eight Princesses
and a Magic Mirror* was a *Guardian*
Book of the Year 2019. *The Tindims and
the Turtle Tangle* is the second
book in the series following
The Tindims of Rubbish Island.

Also by

Sally Gardner & Lydia Corry

The Tindims of Rubbish Island

The TINDIMS

and the Turtle Tangle

Sally Gardner & Lydia Corry

ZEPHYR

an imprint of Head of Zeus

First published in the UK by Zephyr,
an imprint of Head of Zeus, in 2021

9 7 5 3 1 2 4 6 8

A catalogue record for this book is available
from the British Library.

ISBN (PB): 9781838935696
ISBN (E): 9781838935702

Typesetting & design by Jessie Price

Printed and bound in Great Britain
by CPI Group (UK) Ltd, Croydon CR0 4YY

Head of Zeus Ltd
First Floor East
5–8 Hardwick Street
London EC1R 4RG

www.headofzeus.com

To Sylvie
Without whom the
Tindims wouldn't be
half as magical.
With all our love
SG and LC

Chapter One

Where a rather loud noise is heard on Rubbish Island. The kind of noise that doesn't sound right.

'Bad things happen sometimes and that is a fact,' said Pinch.

'Good things happen sometimes as well,' said Skittle.

Brew thought for a moment and said, 'Sometimes both things can happen at the same time, without meaning to.'

And that is where this story starts.

Rubbish Island was bobbing about in
a blue, nothing-could-go-wrong sea. It
was far too hot for any Tindim, worth
his wooden spoon or recycled hat, to be
doing much.

Skittle, Pinch and Brew were at Turtle
Bay building sandcastles, while Ethel B

Dina stood under her sun-stopping, hand-embroidered umbrella. It was the kind of umbrella she felt needed a song.

My umbrella is made for all weather.
Come showers and shine, forever together.

I think my umbrella is second to none.
And I don't care tuppence, if it looks
homespun.
With an umbrella like mine, you are
never alone-'

She was thinking of the next line and
what might rhyme with alone, when she
heard the loudest

GROOOAAN

It was the kind of groan that would make
you stop and ask, 'What was that?'

'Did you hear a loud groan, my still and sparkling darlings?' she asked the others.

Skittle said, 'I heard a **CRACK**.'

'I heard a **SNAP**,' piped up Pinch.

Brew, who was swimming with a turtle, came ashore and said, 'I felt a **RUMBLE** under the water.'

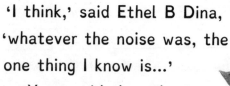

'I think,' said Ethel B Dina, 'whatever the noise was, the one thing I know is...'

'Yes,' said the others all together.

'That it's not the right kind of noise for Rubbish Island to be making.'

They decided to find out if anyone else had heard or felt anything strange.

6

Hitch Stitch was in her garden looking worriedly at a pile of wood.

'Have you heard a groan, my still and sparkling darling?' asked Ethel B Dina.

'I felt a shudder,' said Hitch Stitch. 'And my shed fell down.'

'Oh dear,' they all said.

Pinch said, 'Something seriously serious is wrong and *that's a fact actually.*'

The little party of Tindims set off to
find out what had happened.

Broom's
Orchard

Brew's House
'All-Sorts'

Hitch
Stitch's
House

Bottle
Mountain

Skittle's
House

TURTLE BAY

If anyone knew what the noise meant, it would be Skittle's mum, Admiral Bonnet, and her dad, Captain Spoons. After all, they were in charge of steering the island and making sure it didn't bump into anything.

Today was Winkleday, or as the Long Legs would call it, Wednesday. Granny Gull and Barnacle Bow had come over from their house on Bottle Mountain, to make Roo-Roo jam. This was a special moment in the Tindim calendar. It took a lot of preparation, because jam jars might be small to us Long Legs, but to a Tindim they are much too

big and heavy to move far. So
Roo-Roo jam is always made
at Admiral Bonnet's house.

Each jar was washed out and
scrubbed clean by Barnacle Bow
and decorated and painted by Granny
Gull. She also made the cloth lids which
Hitch Stitch tied around the top of the
jar.

Each one looked as good
as new or, as Granny
Gull would have said,
better for having lived
a bit.

Skittle was sure that nothing horrible could have happened, as long as Roo-Roo jam was being made.

She was about to ask if they had heard anything when there was another loud **SNAP**, followed by a colossal

CRICKETY CLANG

Which all added up to a **VERY BIG NOISE**. The kind of noise no one had ever heard before on Rubbish Island.

'What was that?' said Skittle.

'Search my teabag,' said Brew.

'Something has happened,' said Pinch, 'and *that's a fact.*'

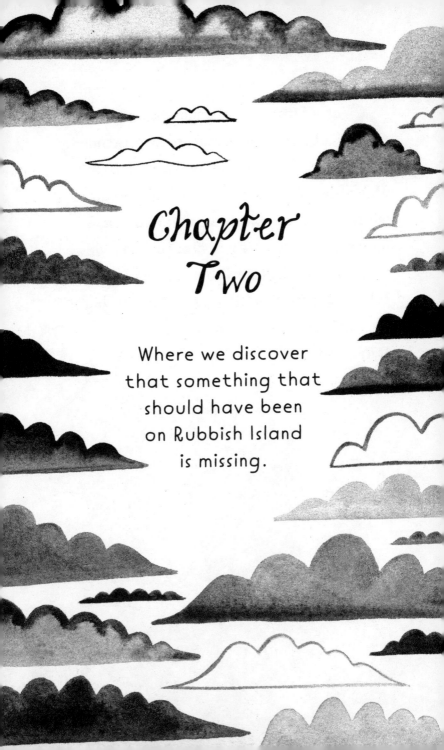

Chapter Two

Where we discover
that something that
should have been
on Rubbish Island
is missing.

One of the main landmarks of Rubbish Island, before the rather loud noise happened, was Bottle Mountain. It loomed like a long shadow, which made the work of steering the island very tricky as it blocked the view.

Over time Bottle Mountain had grown taller and heavier. It had become a big problem that no Tindim wanted to think about.

colourful
plastic bricks

The noise
they heard just
after lunch that
floodtide was
Bottle Mountain
breaking away and
sliding into the sea.
Now, it was bobbing
over the edge of the
world, and with it was
Granny Gull and Barnacle
Bow's house.

plastic bottles hooked
out of the sea

'Oh dear,' said Granny Gull. 'Oh dear, oh deary me. At least none of us were on Bottle Mountain. That is a good thought. Except of course for our dear little house and all that was in our dear little house.'

'We will get it back,' said Barnacle Bow.

'How?' asked Granny Gull.

'How, I don't know,' said
Barnacle Bow. 'But at least it's
shaped like a boat.'

Spokes, who was in charge of
the engine room at the bottom
of the island, came rushing up to
Admiral Bonnet's house.

'Bottle Mountain!' Spokes shouted. 'It's gone.'

'Yes,' they all said.

'I have managed to save the cable car from floating away,' said Spokes.

'Well done,' said Barnacle Bow.

The cable car went from Rubbish Island to Granny Gull's house at the very top of Bottle Mountain. It used to be the fastest way to get from one place to another.

'Never mind,' said Granny Gull bravely. 'Worse things happen at sea. At least we are all safe and sound.'

But somehow Skittle didn't feel that they were.

'Where's Dad?' she asked. 'Where is Captain Spoons?' But no one seemed to be listening.

'Think how much worse this could be,' said Hitch Stitch, 'if anyone had been on Bottle Mountain.'

'Yes,' agreed Ethel B Dina. 'We are lucky that today is Roo-Roo jam making day.'

Chapter Three

Where we find out
that two Tindims are
missing, but why and
who might they be?

Admiral Bonnet was looking out of the kitchen window at Bottle Mountain, fast becoming a dot in the distance.

Just then, there was a knock on the door and to Brew's relief, there was his dad, Jug, and his mum, Mug, holding his baby sister, Cup. They had come to check that everyone had all their bits and bobs.

Spokes said, 'You didn't
happen to see Broom on your
way here?'

Broom was in charge of the
gardens on Rubbish Island. He
was tallest of all the Tindims. In fact,
it would be hard not to see him, even
though he was green.

'No,' said Jug. 'I
thought he would be
here, ready to deliver
the Roo-Roo jam.'

'And have you
seen Captain
Spoons?' asked
Skittle.

'No,' said Mug.
'Your dad,'
said Admiral
Bonnet, 'went

to the library to find a
book on the explorer,
Tiddledim. He's likely
reading down by Turtle Bay.'

'No, Mum,' said Skittle.
'We've been there and we
didn't see Dad.'

'And we didn't see Broom,'
said Jug.

'Oh dear, oh deary me,' said
Granny Gull. 'I have just
remembered something rather
important. Broom went over to
Bottle Mountain to pick the Ting-
a-ling herb and I think Captain
Spoons went with him.'

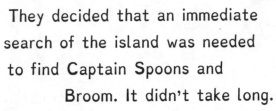

They decided that an immediate
search of the island was needed
to find Captain Spoons and
Broom. It didn't take long.

When they'd finished, Admiral Bonnet said, 'This has turned into a rescue mission. I think Captain Spoons and Broom must both be on Bottle Mountain because we can't find them anywhere else!'

'I knew it,' said Granny Gull. 'Worse things *do* happen at sea.'

Chapter Four

Where Broom and Captain Spoons are blissfully unaware of anything happening, on account of their snoring.

Captain Spoons had helped Broom pick the Ting-a-ling herb until the sun became too hot for tin hats. At floodtide they had gone into Granny Gull's house for a cup of glee and a biscuit. That's tea to you and me.

Broom boiled the kettle. Captain Spoons had found his favourite book on the explorer, Tiddledim, in the library earlier. He was one of the bravest Tindims ever. And he was the only Tindim who had talked to the Long Legs. The Long Legs being you and me, although you would be called the Little Long Legs.

The book had lots of stories about his adventures, which is why Captain Spoons had wanted to read it again.

'Many moons ago,' said Captain Spoons, taking a sip of glee, 'Tiddledim set off from Rubbish Island to find the shores of the Long Legs. He had a simple plan. He was going to tell them not to throw their rubbish into the sea. He came back after making friends with a Little Long Leg.

He decided to go back again to see if the message about rubbish had got through to the Little Long Leg and his friends. And that was the last time anyone saw tin hat or toy whistle of him.'

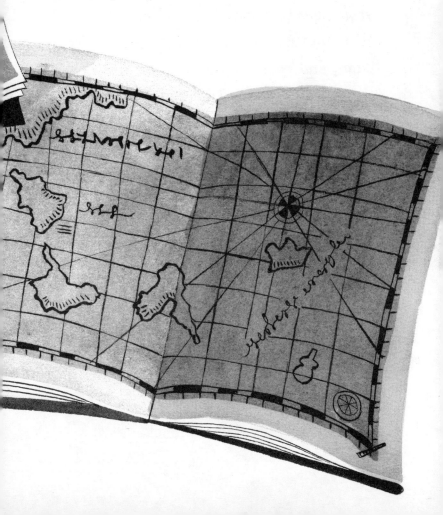

'Then it's a book about the Long Legs. Is that right?' asked Broom, and he yawned.

'Yes, they are a strange bunch, those Long Legs,' said Captain Spoons, also yawning. 'Toothbrushes are important to them,' he said, reading from the first page, and then he yawned again.

'I wonder where Tiddledim is?' said Broom.

Captain Spoons said, 'Drum me a tea tray, I don't know.' And with that they both fell fast asleep.

There is one thing I should say about the Tindims and that is that they snore a lot and very loudly. In fact, a good night's sleep without snoring loudly would worry a Tindim. Captain Spoons and Broom were both making a whale of a racket, so much so that they didn't hear the **GROAN**, the **CRACK**, the **SNAP** or the colossal

CRICKETY
CLANG

They both woke up with a start to find their chairs were resting on the bookshelves and the whole house was topsy-turvy. It was quite a struggle to reach the front door and when they managed to open it, they looked out nervously. Not only was Granny Gull's house on one side, but there was water lapping at the windows.

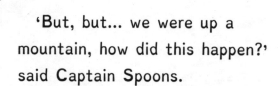

'But, but... we were up a
mountain, how did this happen?'
said Captain Spoons.

'Captain,' said Broom. 'Bottle
Mountain, HAS IT GONE?' Captain
Spoons and Broom looked out of
the window to find themselves
floating in a tangle of plastic
bottles. As for Rubbish Island, it
was a speck on the horizon.

'What are we going to do?' said
Broom.

It was a good question. The
house was beginning to fill with
water.

'I think we're sinking,' said
Captain Spoons.

And just when they thought it
couldn't get any worse, they found
themselves whirling around and
around as more pictures fell off the
wall and ornaments came tumbling
off the mantelpiece.

'Hold on tight,' said Broom, as
the table and chairs began to slide
this way and that. Then the house
righted itself again and the water
drained away.

'It's a good thing that they decided to live on a boat on top of the mountain,' said Captain Spoons.

'You can say that again,' said Broom as they looked out of the window and saw an enormous pair of shoes.

'I don't like the look of those,' said Broom.

'I think,' said Captain Spoons, 'they belong to a Long Leg.'

'Look, there's another smaller pair.'

'I think,' said Captain Spoons, 'they belong to a Little Long Leg.'

'Oh, whistle up windy,' said Broom. 'This is bad. Very bad indeed.'

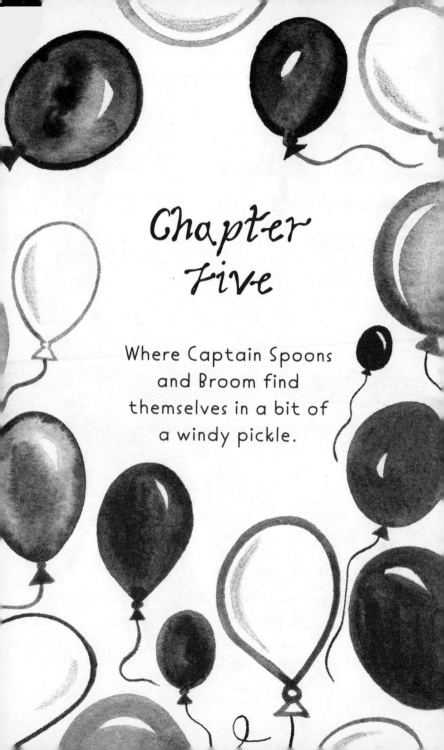

Chapter Five

Where Captain Spoons
and Broom find
themselves in a bit of
a windy pickle.

*N*one of the Tindims had any idea
how tall the Long Legs were.
Captain Spoons had believed they
were smaller than Bottle Mountain. So, it
was a shock when he saw the shoes.

'They are much bigger than I thought,' said Captain Spoons.

They heard the Little Long Leg say, 'Please, Dad, couldn't I keep the houseboat? Look, it has windows and a door.'

'Okay. First we must fish these plastic bottles out of the sea,' said his dad, as he cast huge nets to gather up all the floating bottles.

It took ages, but at last they had
collected the bottles that had been
Bottle Mountain into the net. The Long
Leg carefully attached the houseboat,
so that it could be towed along with the
bottles.

'It's a relief,' said Captain Spoons, 'to
know that these Long Legs are recyclers
like us. It would be a disaster for the fish
if the bottles had been left behind.'

Suddenly, *whoosh*, they found the house going bumpity, bumpity, bump.

'What do you think is happening?' said Broom as the chairs jumped into the air.

It was then they heard the Little Long Leg say, 'Dad, I think you are going too fast. The houseboat might break up in the sea.'

'No, it won't,' said Dad. 'It's safe.'

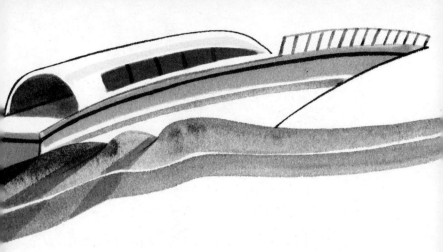

'Safe!' said Broom as the wind blew through the curtains and Broom's fur fluffed up. Sea water sprayed the walls and paintings crashed to the floor again. Broom saw Granny Gull's knickers flying away in the wind. At last they slowed down.

'Maybe it's coming to a stop,' said Captain Spoons.

'About time,' said Broom. 'I hate to think how far away Rubbish Island is now.'

'We will get back,' said Captain Spoons. 'Where there's a spoon and a broom, there's a way.'

Outside everything had changed. Now there was blue sky, sand and trees. Then they were on the move again.

'I think,' said Captain Spoons, 'we are being dragged along in the sand.'

Finally, they came to a stop.

'Where are we?' asked Captain Spoons, picking up his hat.

'I haven't a clue,' said Broom who could see the shoes of the Long Leg and the Little Long Leg, coming and going.

They could hear the Little Long Leg saying, 'Can I play with it now?' every time he went past Granny Gull's house. Until at last the Long Leg said, 'Yes.'

'Wow,' said the Little Long Leg, as he looked in through the window of Granny Gull's house.

'Oh no,' said Broom when he saw the eye of the Little Long Leg. 'They are giants.'

Then the Little Long Leg put his hand through the front door.

That was too much for the Tindims.

'No, no, no,' said Captain Spoons, clapping his hands. 'This will never do.' And bravely he went outside.

The moment the Little Long Leg saw him, he sprang to his feet.

'This houseboat belongs to Granny Gull,' said Captain Spoons. 'It has already been shaken and stirred up enough.'

'Who are you?' asked the Little Long Leg.

'I am Captain Spoons and this is Broom. But we would like to know who *you* are.'

'I am Dylan,' replied the Little Long Leg.

'Very good to meet you,' said Captain Spoons, still feeling brave. 'I need you to promise us that there'll be no more shaking or bumping us about. And that you are not going to recycle Granny Gull's house.'

'Who is Granny Gull?' asked Dylan.

Broom whispered into Captain Spoons' ear, 'I don't think he knows about us.'

Captain Spoons started again. 'Have you never heard of the Tindims?'

Chapter Six

Where Captain Spoons and Broom meet the Little Long Legs and remember something important about turtles.

*D*ylan had never heard of the Tindims or Tiddledim, the explorer. Although he was very pleased to have met Captain Spoons and Broom. And they were impressed at how quickly the Little Long Leg understood the trouble they were in.

'We need to get back to Rubbish Island.'

Dylan explained that they were on a deserted island where turtles lay their eggs. His dad's job was to make sure the turtles hatched safely and made it home to the sea.

The island had a small hut and the Long Legs had put up two tents, so it looked homely.

'My aunt is coming tomorrow to help,' said Dylan. 'And she is bringing my cousin, Maya, with her.'

That evening, as the sun went down, Broom and Captain Spoons sat on a rock looking at the vast ocean. Dylan had kindly brought them a plate of food. Captain Spoons and Broom ate in silence. Both were lost in the same thought. Where, in all that salty water, was Rubbish Island, and how, in a world of recycled plastic cups, would they get back there again?

'This is a beach where turtles hatch,' said Captain Spoons. 'Perhaps all we have to do is talk to a turtle and ask them to pass on a message to Rubbish Island.'

'Well, whistle up windy, that doesn't sound too hard. Do you speak Turtle?' asked Broom.

'No,' said Captain Spoons. 'But I always find that a problem gets smaller after a good night's sleep.'

In the morning, the sun shone brightly, and the sea was a clear blue. They heard the cry of the Little Long Leg and looked round to see three pairs of shoes.

'That's Broom,' he heard the Dylan set of shoes say. 'Dad can't see them.'

'Mum, Mum, come and look,' they heard the other Little Long Leg say.

'Yes,' said the Long Leg, 'what am I supposed to be looking at?'

'The strange thing about the Long Legs,' said Broom to Dylan, 'is that once they're fully grown, they can't see us. Or, so said Tiddledim the explorer.'

'What imaginations you two have,' said Dylan's dad.

'Wait a minute,' said his sister, Maya's mum. 'That reminds me. When we were little, didn't you used to have a friend called Middlebin, or was it Thimbledim?'

'No.'

'Yes, you did,' she said 'oh, I remember now, it was Tiddledim.'

'Well I don't remember,' replied the Long Leg.

'Well, blow my tin hat into a trumpet, did I just hear what I thought I heard?' said Captain Spoons. He started to dance a jig. 'You know what this means.'

'Yes,' said Broom. 'He must have once met Tiddledim the explorer.'

Chapter Seven

Where Pinch comes up
with an idea of how
to rescue Captain
Spoons and Broom.

*B*ack on Rubbish Island, everyone was trying to think how best to rescue Captain Spoons and Broom.

Admiral Bonnet had been looking at maps and charts. 'Bottle Mountain is bound to be somewhere,' she said. 'It's just where that somewhere is.'

Skittle said, 'This is a pickle.'

Brew said, 'Too true.'

Pinch said, 'What about making a kite? Perhaps if we wrote on it, we could ask the birds to keep a look out.'

Skittle thought that was an excellent idea. The three of them went to work, drawing their ideas for a kite.

'It doesn't look much like a kite,' said
Brew looking at Pinch's drawing.

Skittle gave Brew a nudge.

'Oh,' said Brew. 'I see what it is. I was
looking at the drawing upside down and
now it's a, a, a...'

'A kite in the shape of a purrtle,' said Pinch.

'What's a purrtle?' asked Brew.

'A purrtle is a very rare bird, with two r's and *that's a fact actually*,' said Pinch.

Skittle thought Spokes should look at Pinch's drawing. Spokes scratched his head.

'This is a purrtle, with two r's, if ever I saw one,' he said.

'Yes,' said Pinch. 'Spokes knows what it is.'

Spokes thought for a minute and said:

'You wouldn't want your purrtle
Mistaken for a turtle.
For a turtle can't hurtle
But a purrtle can.'

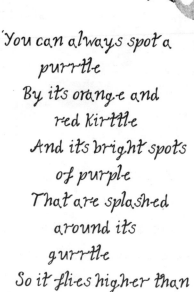

'That's a fact,' said Pinch.

'You can always spot a
purrtle
By its orange and
red kirtle
And its bright spots
of purple
That are splashed
around its
gurrtle
So it flies higher than
a Yurrtle.

58

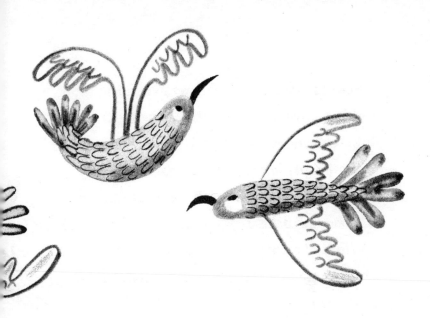

No do not mistake a purrtle
Just because it doesn't look right
For a purrtle is perfect for a kite.'

'Wow,' said Brew.

And before you could say,
'Roo-Roo jam tarts,'
Spokes decided that
Pinch's drawing would
make the best kite of
all.

Skittle, Pinch and Brew spent the morning covering the kite with paper and glue. On one side, Skittle painted, in bright purple paint, *Help! Bottle Mountain missing*. On the other, *Help! Captain Spoons and Broom missing*.

When the kite was finished Pinch said, 'That is just what a purrtle with two r's looks like.'

'No one has seen a purrtle for a long, long time. Perhaps they are extinct now,' said Brew.

'That's the whole point,' said Pinch. 'Other birds will be so pleased to see a purrtle, with two r's, that they will read our cry for help. And *that's a fact.*'

Pinch felt rather proud of himself for coming up with such a good idea. They stood, waiting for a gust of wind.

The first gust came and the kite didn't fly.

'Blasted bottle tops,' said Skittle.

Hitch Stitch, who was a champion kite flyer, came to help. She said, 'It's not wind, it's hot air you need.' And she showed them what to do.

'Me, me, let me,' said Pinch. 'After all, it was my idea.'

Which was true. He took the string in his mouth and was surprised to find himself going steadily upwards. Hitch Stitch had to use her useful hook to catch hold of him.

By teatime, Skittle, Pinch and Brew's tummies were rumbling. A delicious smell wafted towards them, which made all of them very hungry indeed. It was making them think of Roo-Roo jam tarts instead of kites.

'Have you noticed,' said Brew, 'not many birds have looked at our kite? I'm wondering if birds can read?'

'I'm not sure,' said Skittle. 'I don't think they can.'

'Shall we go and have tea?' said Pinch.

It was in between him saying, 'Shall we' and 'go and have tea?', that all three of them, without meaning to, let go of the string. The kite flew away into the clouds.

'Purrtle a turtle, what now?' said Brew.

Chapter Eight

Where that teatime,
the talk is all of
turtles, kites and the
best way to bring
Captain Spoons and
Broom home.

Teatime is the Tindims' favourite part of the day. It needs to be done properly with 'a stiff upper lip,' as that is what Granny Gull had read on a page of a washed-up magazine. She had no idea what a stiff upper lip was.

Admiral Bonnet said, 'It must be one of the many things the Long Legs say, that makes not a plastic straw of sense.'

Barnacle Bow thought it might be to do with rock cakes. Perhaps without a stiff upper lip, the Long Legs wouldn't be able

to eat rock cakes for tea.

'Why would you want to eat a rock
cake in the first place,' said Spokes,
'when there are Granny Gull's Roo-Roo
jam tarts?'

It was a question, sharp as a needle
and without the thread of an answer.
But then again, there were so many
words that the Long Legs used that the
Tindims didn't understand. Like 'still' and
'sparkling' which they found written on
plastic bottle labels.

'How is the kite
flying going?' asked Spokes.
'It went all right,' said Skittle.
'Then it went all wrong,' said Brew.
'How did it go wrong?' asked Spokes.
'The kite sort of flew away,' said
Pinch, 'when we let go of the string.'

'And we don't think birds can read, so
it wasn't much help,' said Brew.

'You don't know,' said Spokes. 'It
might still be up there and someone might
find it and read it.'

Barnacle Bow filled up the gleepot again and Ethel B Dina, who had eaten four jam tarts, told them she had twelve baby turtles in her fish hospital. They had hatched on a distant island. There had been two hundred and sixty eggs, but the beach had so much litter on it that many of the baby turtles didn't know which way the sea was. Then there were the crabs and not to mention the hungry gulls. After all that, there weren't many baby turtles left.

They talked about the turtles and about how they might find Captain Spoons and Broom. In fact, they talked and talked until all the Roo-Roo jam tarts were gone.

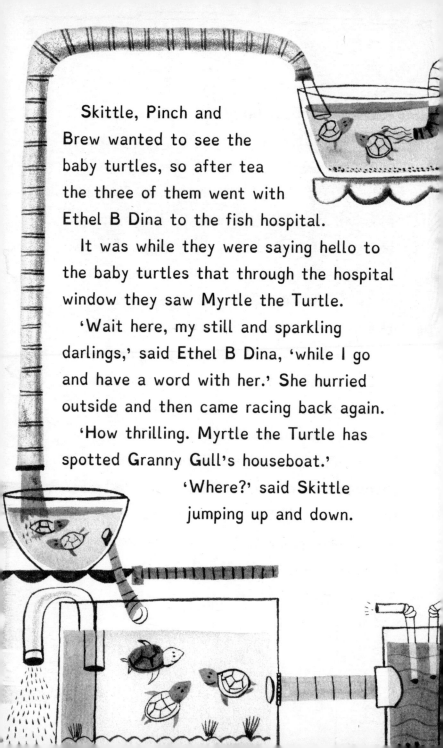

Skittle, Pinch and Brew wanted to see the baby turtles, so after tea the three of them went with Ethel B Dina to the fish hospital.

It was while they were saying hello to the baby turtles that through the hospital window they saw Myrtle the Turtle.

'Wait here, my still and sparkling darlings,' said Ethel B Dina, 'while I go and have a word with her.' She hurried outside and then came racing back again.

'How thrilling. Myrtle the Turtle has spotted Granny Gull's houseboat.'

'Where?' said Skittle jumping up and down.

'On a sandy beach of
Turtle Island, where all her
lady friends lay their eggs.
She's very upset to hear that
there are only twelve baby
turtles here. She thought there
would have been at least a hundred.
Come on we'd better go and tell
Admiral Bonnet.'

71

Chapter Nine

Where we find Broom and Captain Spoons going to work to clean up the beach. And Captain Spoons has a battle with a crab.

C aptain Spoons and Broom woke early next morning. As there was no one about, they went to investigate the island.

'I can see sand,' said Broom, 'and a lot of it.'

'I can see rubbish,' said Captain Spoons, 'and a lot of it.'

As they walked along the beach they thought it was rather sad that there were so many useful things thrown away, as if they were no use. Most of what they found could have been made into something handy and different.

cans

'One thing
is certain,' said
Captain Spoons.
'The Long Legs have
never heard our motto:

Rubbish today
is treasure
tomorrow.

plastic bottles
everywhere

straws

'No,' said
Broom. 'What I don't
understand is why would
you want to throw all this
away in the first place?'
Captain Spoons
scratched his head and
said, 'Catch me a kipper,
I don't know.'

springs
and things

'I think we should do what we always do,' said Broom.

The Tindims have a way of doing things. First, they look for treasure, then they make three piles — treasure, useful and nearly useful things.

All this they did with great speed because the Tindims are born recyclers. If you were to ask them, they would say the word 'rubbish' is wrong. That perhaps it is the most misunderstood word ever. To them rubbish means all sorts of things that can be made into all sorts of other useful things.

NEARLY USEFUL

USEFUL

TREASURE

'Look at this,' said Captain Spoons,
'a sword. It is just my size and it's been
thrown away.'

Broom couldn't look as he was being
chased by a crab. He shouted, 'Captain,
come quick and bring that sword.'

'Blow me a trumpet, what's going on?'
said Captain Spoons.

'Baby turtles,' shouted Broom. 'And a
hungry crab.'

Captain Spoons charged down the
beach and fought off the crab while
Broom bent down and picked up as many
baby turtles as he could and took them
to the sea. Finally, the crab gave up and
stalked off in a sulk.

'They must have hatched last night,'
said Captain Spoons. 'And in all the
rubbish they couldn't find the sea.'

They had been working for some time when they saw Dylan and Maya walking towards them.

'Over here, we need help finding the baby turtles,' shouted Broom.

'That is the second nest we've missed. Dad will be upset,' said Dylan.

'Don't worry about that now,' said Captain Spoons. 'It's all hands to the rescue!'

Once Dylan and Maya started to help, they managed to scoop up as many little turtles as they could spot and take them to the sea.

'Hey, guys,' said Maya's mum, 'we've been calling you for breakfast.'

She stopped, surprised to see a good part of the rubbish on the beach had been put into three neat piles.

'Did you do this?' she said. 'That's brilliant.'

'No,' said Dylan. 'The Tindims did it.'

'If it hadn't been for Captain Spoons and Broom, the baby turtles would be lost,' said Maya.

'Is that so?' said Maya's mum.

That's when she saw a baby turtle hovering above the ground. What she couldn't see was Broom holding the baby turtle above his head and striding towards the sea.

Maya's mum said, 'My eyes are playing tricks. I'm seeing flying turtles.'

Chapter Ten

Where we find that
birds might not be able
to read what is written
on the kite, although
the Long Legs can.

The Long Legs had put a table under the shade of a palm tree, because it was already getting hot.

'I think,' said Broom to Captain Spoons, 'it is rude to have your sword at the table.'

'I know, but I am a bit worried about the crab snatching it.'

Just then, they all looked up as a small kite fell out of the palm tree and landed in one of the Long Legs' cereal bowls.

The Little Long Legs asked, 'What is it?'

'I am not sure, I think it's a kite,' said Dad.

Then he burst out laughing, 'That's
good. Did you two do this?'

Before the Little Long Legs could say
anything, Captain Spoons had climbed
onto the table.

'Manners be blowed,' said Broom and
he followed Spoons.

'Can I see the kite, please?' said
Captain Spoons to the Long Legs.

'Dad,' said Dylan, 'Captain Spoons
wants to see the kite. And no, I didn't
make it and neither did Maya.'

Dad stared at the kite that appeared to be floating above the table. Dylan couldn't understand what was wrong with his aunt and Dad. 'Why can't you see them?'

'Because there's no one there,' said Dad.

'I don't think I ever want to grow up, if it means I won't be able to see a Tindim,' said Dylan.

'Do you know,' said his dad, 'I felt that too when I thought I would never see Tiddledim the explorer again. And then one day he disappeared.'

'Did you hear that?' said Captain Spoons to Broom. 'He *did* know Tiddledim.'

'All right,' said Maya's mum. 'Let's settle this. I want to see if you're playing tricks. Kids, stand well back. If Captain Spoons is there' — she thought for a moment — 'he can tap the cereal box three times.'

Captain Spoons picked up his sword and tapped the box three times.

'Wow,' said Maya's mum.

'We told you,' said the Little Long Legs.

'Okay,' said Dylan's dad. 'Do you happen to know where Tiddledim the explorer is? Tap once for yes and twice for no.'

Captain Spoons tapped twice and then said, 'This is silly. Just tell your dad we don't have Tiddledim. We wish we did. But we do have his book.'

They waited while Broom went back to Granny Gull's house to fetch the book. The Long Legs looked in wonder, as a tiny book floated towards them.

Dylan's dad picked it up. At the back was a drawing of a pair of legs and next to them was a bird.

'That's me when I was your age,' he said, 'and the bird was Tiddledim's travelling companion. It's a purrtle with two r's.'

Whether or not it was because the Long Leg had remembered Tiddledim the explorer was hard to say, but that day, clearing up the rubbish was done in a whizz.

By the time the sun was setting, the beach was shiny, salty sand all the way down to the sea. The rubbish had been labelled, ready to be taken off the island when they left.

'Now all we have to do,' said the Long Leg, 'is wait for the turtles' eggs to hatch.'

'And let's hope there is a turtle who might be able to take a message to Rubbish Island,' said Captain Spoons.

Chapter Eleven

Where we find Admiral Bonnet getting ready with the help of Jug to set off on a rescue mission. And Spokes shows off his new boat.

'Wait an anchor,' said Admiral Bonnet. 'Did you say Myrtle the Turtle was here?'

'Yes,' said Ethel B Dina. 'She thinks she saw Granny Gull's house on Turtle Island.'

'What happened to Bottle Mountain?' asked Admiral Bonnet.

'And where is Turtle Island?' asked Jug.

She hurried to get her charts and maps again. Jug and Admiral Bonnet studied them carefully. By Jug's calculations, Turtle Island wasn't that far away.

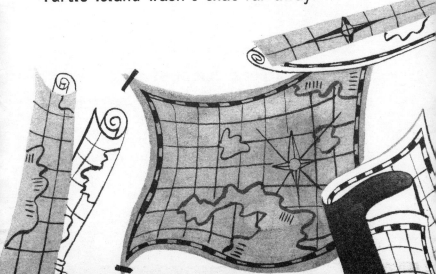

The Tindims decided that Admiral
Bonnet should go to the island to save
the others. Admiral Bonnet was sure she
could get there and be back by teatime
tomorrow.

'My still and sparkling darlings, there is
more that I want to say,' said Ethel.

But Admiral Bonnet wasn't listening as
she set off down the steps towards the
jetty.

She found Spokes putting the finishing
touches to a boat that he'd made out of
the rescued cable car. It was just the
right size to be turned into a tug boat
and strong enough for a rescue mission.

He had made the engine work by using
an elastic band which he had wound up as
tight as it would go. All Admiral Bonnet
had to do was push the 'go' switch and
the boat would speed off.

93

'Now that is what I call a sturdy,
seaworthy vessel, if ever I saw one,'
said Admiral Bonnet, rubbing her hands
together. 'Strong enough for a rescue
mission. Has it, by any chance, a rhyme
to go with it? After all, every boat needs
a poem to bring it luck,' she added.

'As it happens, I do have one up my
sleeve,' said Spokes.

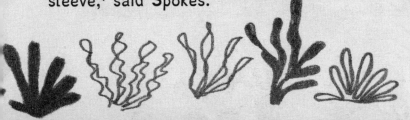

'I have turned the chair lift into a boat
With extra bounce to keep it afloat.
There is a red sail, if there's wind about
And a compass on board, in case of doubt.
I have packed you a picnic and a flask
    of glee
To keep away hunger while you're at
    sea.
It will speed along – there shouldn't be
    a hitch.
When you're ready to set off, just hit
    the switch.'

'Is that it?' said Admiral Bonnet. 'It
needs to end with a more upbeat line,
like:

"This boat is sturdy, excellent and true.
And I know it will look after you."'

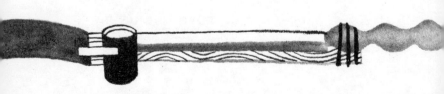

96

'That will do,' said Spokes. You'll have guessed by now that, as well as songs, the Tindims were rather good at making up poems.

Just as Admiral Bonnet put her foot on the ladder to climb aboard, Skittle, Pinch and Brew came bowling down the steps onto the jetty.

Pinch was trying to catch a ball that
Skittle had thrown for him. Except it had
gone too high and landed in the boat.

'Oh, soggy teabags,' said Brew.

'I'll get it,' said Admiral Bonnet.

By now she was halfway down the
ladder. Pinch didn't stop to think and
jumped aboard. Spokes tried to stop

him, but he missed and tripped over the
rope that was attached to the ladder,
which meant Admiral Bonnet landed
back on the jetty. Then Pinch, without
knowing what he had done, hit the 'go'
switch with the tip of his tail. Before you
could say 'Whistle up windy', the boat
had zoomed off across the water.

On the jetty stood a somewhat stunned Admiral Bonnet, a baffled Spokes and a bewildered Brew and Skittle.

'That wasn't meant to happen,' said Admiral Bonnet. 'There isn't a line in the rhyme for a disaster like that.'

'Stew me a tea bag,' said Brew, as he watched the boat disappear.

'What will happen to Pinch?' said Skittle.

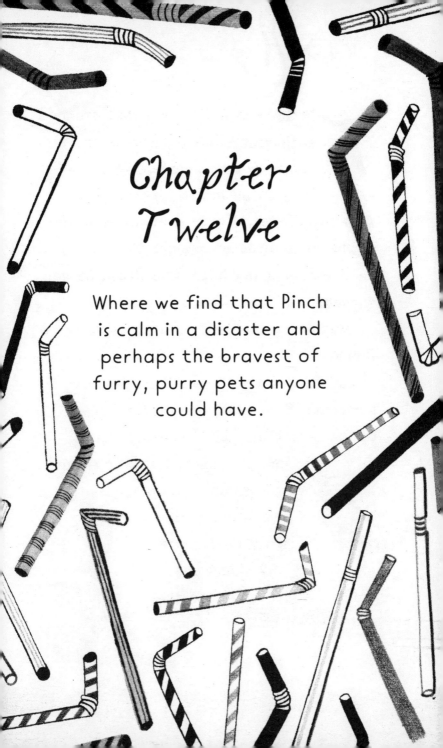

Chapter Twelve

Where we find that Pinch is calm in a disaster and perhaps the bravest of furry, purry pets anyone could have.

The boat moved with such speed, all Pinch could do was watch as Rubbish Island disappeared in the great blue sea. And then, when he was in the middle of nowhere, everything stopped. The rubber band that was making the engine work snapped and the power was gone.

'This is a pickle and no mistake,' said Pinch.

But he'd learned there is no point panicking. Something good often comes out of something bad. He found the red sail, the compass, the glee and the sandwiches which made everything a little better. He ate the sandwiches, drank the glee and used the sail to keep himself warm.

Then he curled up, watched the stars, and let the sea gently rock him to sleep.

Next neeptide the sea was as flat as an ironed tea towel. As for the cable car boat, it had become tangled in something.

Pinch looked over the side and saw that it was caught up in a whole load of old fishing nets that had been dumped in the sea.

Now this tangled mess was floating
around and causing a lot of trouble,
because among the nets and bottles were
hundreds of trapped tiny baby turtles.
Something needed to be done and quickly.

'Don't panic,' said Pinch as he wrapped
his long tail around the mast of the boat.
Then he hung upside down and tried to
free as many of the baby turtles as he
could.

What he would have given to have
hands rather than paws. Untangling
turtles with paws and teeth is tricky
work.

The baby turtles he managed to free,
he put safely in the boat. The turtles big
enough to swim away, he put back
into the sea.

Pinch had been working so hard that he hadn't been paying attention to where the boat and the knotted netting were heading. He looked up to see...

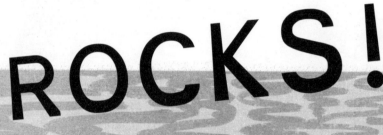

ROCKS!

Pinch couldn't think
what to do for the
best. What would Skittle
say? He thought she might say, 'How do
you manage a pile of recycled bottles?
One bottle at a time.'

First, he carried
on freeing all the
turtles he could
reach. But he would
have to leave the boat to help the
others. The rocks were getting
closer.

Bravely Pinch unwound
his tail and climbed onto the
tangled mess. It felt horribly soggy.
He was carefully making his way towards
more trapped turtles when he saw Myrtle
the Turtle swimming nearby. She looked
worried.

'We are in big trouble,' said Pinch.
'This is a proper turtle tangle and
that's a fact!'

Chapter
Thirteen

Where Captain Spoons and Broom meet Myrtle the Turtle, who tells them about the turtle tangle.

*B*ack on the beach, the Long Legs and the Little Long Legs were having a lazy morning. They'd been up most of the night, making sure the baby turtles had found their way down to the sea. There had been several clashes with crabs and the Long Legs had chased the gulls away. All in all, it had been a great success.

So it was a little puzzling, while the Long Legs and the Little Long Legs were eating a well-earned breakfast, to see a large turtle crawling up the beach.

Captain Spoons and Broom rushed to greet Myrtle the Turtle.

'Good neeptide to you,' said Captain Spoons.

Then he realised that Myrtle didn't understand a word he was saying. Which was a pity because Myrtle the Turtle had a lot to say. Broom thought they should see if Tiddledim's book had any hints on how to speak Turtle.

'What's going on?' asked Dylan, seeing Captain Spoons and Broom trying to talk Turtle.

'We are hoping that Myrtle might tell us what's worrying her,' said Captain Spoons.

'Oh,' said Dylan. 'Can you speak to a turtle?'

'No. But we have Tiddledim's book,' said Broom, who had managed to work out what Myrtle was saying.

Broom said, 'I think it goes something like this, Myrtle the Turtle says it's all a fang-dangle. In other words, a proper turtle tangle.'

'What does that mean?' asked Captain Spoons.

Broom listened carefully to Myrtle.

'I think,' said Broom, 'what she's trying to say, is that she's seen Pinch on a boat. The boat is stuck in a lot of old rubbish and all the newly hatched turtles are tangled in it and are stuck too. The whole thing is about to hit the rocks.'

'Wait, did you say Pinch?' asked Captain Spoons.

'Yes,' said Broom. 'And I said rocks.'

'That's terrible,' said Captain Spoons. 'What's he doing there? Is he alone?'

'Myrtle says that Admiral Bonnet was going to come and rescue us. But Pinch jumped into the boat and pressed the 'go' switch.'

'What boat? What switch? Panic!' shouted Captain Spoons. 'Rocks! No, I mean, HELP!' He ran up to Dylan.

'Help! Pinch is out there all by himself.'

Dylan looked out to sea. 'Who's Pinch?' he asked.

'My daughter's furry, purry pet. He is trying to save the baby turtles who are all in a fang-dangle, no I mean in a turtle tangle.'

'What's happening?' asked Maya, who had come to join them.

Broom had Captain Spoons' telescope. He could just make out something large, floating in the sea.

'Yes, I see it too,' said Dylan. 'Quick!
Go and get Dad.'

Maya rushed to tell the Long Legs that
the baby turtles were in danger. When
the Long Legs saw the tangled mess for
themselves, they knew what had happened
straight away and pushed their boat out
to sea.

Dylan climbed onboard with Captain Spoons and Maya took Broom. The Long Legs were surprised to see the large turtle was following them.

'She's called Myrtle,' said Dylan.

'Is she?' said Dad, laughing.

'That's what Captain Spoons says.'

'Oh dear,' said Captain Spoons, as he looked through the telescope. Among the tangled mess, he spied the cable car from Bottle Mountain, but he couldn't see Pinch.

'I can see Pinch,' said Broom.

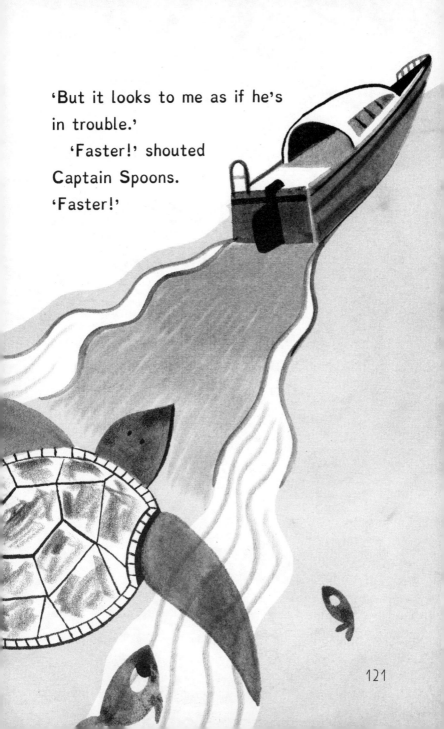

'But it looks to me as if he's
in trouble.'
    'Faster!' shouted
Captain Spoons.
'Faster!'

121

Chapter Fourteen

Where the Long Legs and the Little Long Legs go to the rescue. But are they too late?

inch had begun to sink in between the rubbish. The more he tried to free himself, the worse the sinking became. Beneath him he could feel something roundish and warm that was keeping him afloat.

Perhaps, he thought, it hadn't been such a good idea to climb onto the nets. Just then, a huge wave splashed over him and he thought that they might have hit the rocks, when a large pair of hands pulled the tangled mess out of the sea.

It took Pinch a few minutes to realise three things. First, he was now on a firm, dry surface. Second, the thing that had been keeping him afloat was actually an egg. Third, and best of all, he had found Broom and Captain Spoons.

Pinch was so pleased to see them that he jumped into Captain Spoons' arms.

Then he saw the Little Long Legs.

'They are giants,' he said. 'And *that's a fact actually.*'

'Friendly giants,' said Captain Spoons. 'They will help us get home.'

After all the baby
turtles had been freed and
returned safely to the sea, the
Long Legs set about packing up the
nets and rubbish so that it couldn't
do any more harm to turtles or fish.

They were going to take the rubbish
back to the mainland to be recycled
when they left. Now the only problem
was how to get the Tindims home again.

The Long Legs sat at the table under
the palm tree and studied the cable
car boat.

'What a brilliant design,' they
said.

'All it needs is a new rubber
band.'

Dylan explained
to Dad that Captain
Spoons needed the cable
car boat to be strong enough
to tow Granny Gull's houseboat
back to Rubbish Island.

'The best thing of all,' said Captain
Spoons, 'is there's no more Bottle
Mountain. So now when I steer
Rubbish Island, I will be able to see
where I am going.'

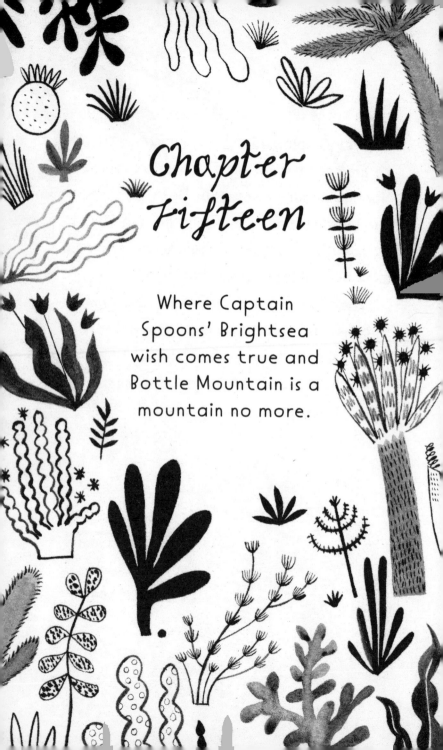

Chapter Fifteen

Where Captain
Spoons' Brightsea
wish comes true and
Bottle Mountain is a
mountain no more.

While Captain Spoons was busy with Bottle Mountain, Pinch sat next to Broom, on a rock, drying his fur in the sun. Both of them wondered what kind of egg he had found.

'I don't think it will hatch,' said Broom. 'It's been in the water too long.'

Pinch had his tail curled around the egg, to keep it warm. 'I'm sure it will be all right,' he said.

'Perhaps,' said Broom, 'there might be something about it in Tiddledim's book.'

Broom flicked through the pages until he reached a chapter on the rare beasts and birds of Rubbish Island.

BLUE BUG

'There's the blue bug and the tranter-squealer, thought to be extinct,' said Broom.

'What's that?' said Pinch.

Broom showed him a picture of a small, lizard creature.

'I have never seen one of those,' he said.

'Then there is the purrtle, with two r's,' said Broom. 'Purrtles often lay their eggs in the oddest of places.'

TRANTER SQUEALER

PURRTLE

PURRTLE EGG

Purrtles (with two r's) often lay their eggs in the oddest of places

They were both pondering this when Captain Spoons came to find them.

'The Long Legs have done it,' he said.

'Done what?' said Broom and Pinch together.

'Made the cable car boat work.'

'Does that mean we can go home?' asked Pinch.

On the shoreline Dylan's dad had the tug boat waiting to set sail with Granny Gull's houseboat neatly tied to it. Everyone climbed aboard.

Dylan's dad said, 'Although I can't see you, I know the Tindims are real. I would just like to tell you, it was due to Tiddledim the explorer, that I decided to work as a conservationist. To do my best to stop people from throwing rubbish into the sea.'

'Dad,' said Dylan, 'is that true?'

'Yes,' said his dad.

Captain Spoons said, 'Thank you. We hope one day we will find Tiddledim the explorer. Don't worry, we will get home. After all, we have the turtles to help.'

'What did they say?' asked Dad.

Dylan told his dad. The Long Legs looked up. There was a line of turtles as far as the eye could see. They were there to help guide the little boat home.

It was a sad and happy farewell, as
farewells often are. Broom and Pinch
waved goodbye, as Captain Spoons flicked
the 'go' switch and they set off for home.
They were going quite fast and it didn't
take long before Rubbish Island came into
view.

'It does look odd without Bottle
Mountain,' said Broom.

'It won't take long,' said Captain
Spoons, 'before it's there again. Of that
I am sure, just as sure as I am of my tin
hat.'

135

It was as they were coming into Turtle Bay that Pinch said, 'Oh no, the egg has cracked. I was being so careful too.'

Broom burst out laughing. 'No, Pinch, it's hatched, look!' And there was the sweetest baby chick.

'Do you know,' said Pinch, 'sometimes bad things happen that turn out to be a lot better than you think.'

There was quite a party on Rubbish Island the night the Tindims arrived home. After all, they had such a lot to celebrate. Not least that Pinch had brought back the rarest of chicks.

As he said, 'It's a purrtle with two r's and *that's a fact!*'

'Rubbish today is treasure tomorrow.'

MAKE A FISH OUT OF A PLASTIC BOTTLE

You will need: an empty plastic bottle, cardboard, sellotape, paint, your imagination.

Take an empty plastic bottle and ask your Long Leg to help you cut it in half. Then on the cardboard, draw a fish tail shape and cut it out. Sellotape the tail to the bottom of the bottle and now you have a fish. Decorate however you like!

Help keep beaches clean! Tell the Long Legs to pick up litter and take it home!